STUART LITTLE™

Stuart Hides Out

story by Susan Hill

pictures by Lydia Halverson

HarperCollins*Publishers*

Stuart Hides Out
™ & © 2001 by Columbia Pictures Industries, Inc. All Rights Reserved
Story by Susan Hill
Illustrations by Lydia Halverson
Printed in the U.S.A. All rights reserved.
www.harperchildrens.com

Library of Congress Cataloging-in-Publication Data
Hill, Susan.
  Stuart hides out / story by Susan Hill ; pictures by Lydia Halverson.
    p.   cm. — (An I can read book)
  Summary: When Stuart Little and Snowbell the cat are left alone for the afternoon, they
discover that the game of hide-and-seek can be dangerous.
  ISBN 0-06-029536-8 — ISBN 0-06-029634-8 (lib. bdg.) — ISBN 0-06-444301-9 (pbk.)
  [1. Mice—Fiction.   2. Cats—Fiction.   3. Hide-and-seek—Fiction.]
I. Halverson, Lydia, ill.   II. Title.   III. Series.
PZ7.H5574 St 2001   00-061382
[E]—dc21

❖

STUART LITTLE™

Stuart Hides Out

One day Stuart Little's mother,

father, and brother, George, went out.

Stuart was left alone

with the family cat, Snowbell.

"I guess it's just you and me,

Snowbell," said Stuart.

"Oh joy," said Snowbell.

"We could have fun together,"
Stuart said. "You know,
like friends do."

"Please," said Snowbell.

"I don't eat you for lunch.

That is as friendly as I get

with a mouse."

"Let's play a game,"

said Stuart.

Snowbell yawned.

"Checkers? Parcheesi?"

said Stuart.

"How about a nice game

of hide-and-seek,"

Snowbell said.

"You hide, I'll seek."

"Hide-and-seek it is,"
said Stuart. "Close your eyes
and count to one hundred!"
"You bet," Snowbell said.

He closed his eyes.

He fell asleep.

Stuart tried a few hiding places.

Then he saw a flower vase

high on a shelf.

"That is a good hiding place,"

Stuart said.

He climbed up onto the shelf

and slid down into the vase.

He sat down to wait.

"Snowbell will never find me!"

Stuart said.

After a while, Stuart said,

"It's not very comfortable in here."

After another while, Stuart said,

"This game used to be more fun."

18

Finally Stuart said,

"I think I'm the only one playing."

Stuart stretched his arms up.

He could not reach the top of the vase.

"Oh, no!" cried Stuart.

"I'm stuck in here!"

Snowbell woke up and stretched.

"I guess old Stuart

has learned a lesson.

The mouse can't win

in a cat-and-mouse game."

After a while, Snowbell said,
"I hope he doesn't hide
for too long."
After another while, Snowbell said,
"Wait. What am I doing
even thinking about the mouse?"

Finally Snowbell said,

"I've really got to get out more."

"Nobody will ever find me in here,"
Stuart said.

"I have to tip the vase over

so I can crawl out."

Stuart began to rock back and forth.

The vase tipped to one side.

It tipped to the other side.

Then it fell over and began to roll

faster and faster toward

the edge of the shelf!

"Whoa!" Stuart cried.

"Maybe I'll just have
a small snack before going out,"
said Snowbell.
"Help!" Stuart yelled.

Snowbell looked up

and saw the vase rolling fast.

"Stuart!" shouted Snowbell.

28

He jumped onto the shelf
and pounced on the vase
just in time.

Stuart crawled out of the vase.

"Snowbell, you found me!"

cried Stuart.

"Well, I wanted a snack,

and that made me think of you,"

said Snowbell.

"Thanks for saving me," Stuart said.

"Keep it to yourself, Mouse-Boy.
This kind of cat-and-mouse game
gets no respect," said Snowbell.

"No problem, Snow,"
said Stuart.

"But next time,

I get to choose the game!"